KU-542-072

This ELMER book belongs to:

. . . .

34 4124 0001 1099

For Gillian and Eric Hill

This paperback edition first published in 2011 by Andersen Press Ltd.
First published in Great Britain in 2010 by Andersen Press Ltd.,
20 Vauxhall Bridge Road, London SW1V 2SA.
Published in Australia by Random House Australia Pty.,
Level 3, 100 Pacific Highway, North Sydney, NSW 2060.
Copyright © David McKee, 2010
The rights of David McKee to be identified as the author and illustrator
of this work have been asserted by him in accordance with
the Copyright, Designs and Patents Act, 1988.
All rights reserved.
Colour separated in Switzerland by Photolitho AG, Zürich.
Printed and bound in Singapore by Tien Wah Press.
David McKee has used gouache in this book.

10   9   8   7   6   5   4   3   2   1

British Library Cataloguing in Publication Data available.

ISBN 978 1 84939 243 3

This book has been printed on acid-free paper

ELMER
and Papa Red

David McKee

Andersen Press

Elmer, the patchwork elephant, smiled. It was two days before the annual visit of Papa Red. The young elephants were excited.

"Take them for a walk, Elmer," said an older elephant. "Then we can prepare the presents in peace."

"Come on, youngsters," Elmer called. "We'll go and get the tree."
Squealing with laughter, the young elephants hurried after Elmer.

"Are we going to where Papa Red lives?" they asked.
"Close by," said Elmer.
"Have you seen him, Elmer?"
Elmer smiled. "Yes," he said. For the rest of the walk
they asked Elmer about Papa Red.

The walk went up and up. The jungle became pine trees. Then, for the first time in their lives, the youngsters saw snow. Papa Red was forgotten.

Elmer left the young ones to play in the snow and
went to choose a tree. "Hello, Elmer," said a moose.
"Let them see Papa Red tomorrow but keep them
hidden. We'll have a busy night ahead."
"I know," said Elmer. "We won't bother you."

Elmer chose a tree that would be easy to put back later.
The youngsters helped to carry it. By now it was late.
"Straight to bed when we get home," said Elmer. "We
have a lot to do tomorrow."

The next day everyone helped to decorate the tree. "The presents, the presents!" shouted the young elephants.

The presents, wrapped and decorated, were placed around the tree. When it was finished the other animals came to admire it.
"Wonderful," they said.

That night, when the big elephants were asleep, or pretending to be, Elmer collected the youngsters together. "This is your chance to see Papa Red," he said. "Hide where you can see but not be seen."

The youngsters had just hidden, when, from out of the sky, came six moose, pulling a sleigh with Papa Red aboard. They landed, and Elmer helped load the presents into the sleigh. "Thanks, Elmer," said Papa Red. Then he winked. "I'm glad we weren't seen."

Papa Red flew off
and the young ones rushed out.
"We saw him, we saw him!" they shouted. "He
took the presents." Elmer laughed and said, "This is
the season for giving. We give and Papa Red takes the
presents to whoever needs them the most."

Once all the elephants were finally asleep, Elmer
tiptoed among them. By each young elephant he
placed a present that Papa Red had left for them.
Elmer smiled. "Good old Papa Red," he said.

Read more ELMER stories

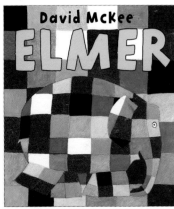
9781842707319 Also available as a book and CD

9781842707500 Also available as a book and CD

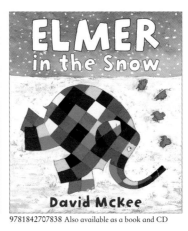
9781842707838 Also available as a book and CD

9781842709504 Also available as a book and CD

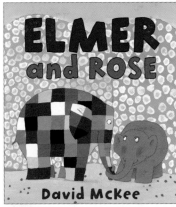
9781842707401

9781842708385 Also available as a book and CD

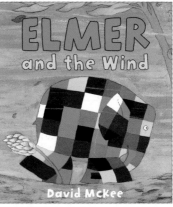
9781842707739 Also available as a book and CD

9781842707494 Also available as a book and CD

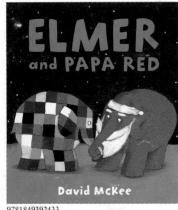
9781849392433

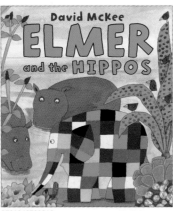
9781842709818

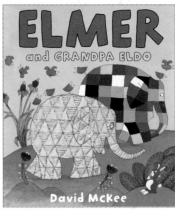
9781842708392

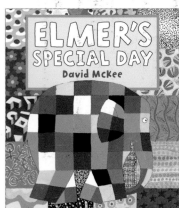
9781842709856

Find out more about David McKee and Elmer, visit:
www.andersenpress.co.uk/elmer